CHELLYFISH AND THE TURTLE

Tales of an Ocean Girl

Michael Fegan

Illustrated by Maggie Cummins and Meredith Rae

CONTENTS

For Chellyfish
For Always

Chellyfish And The Turtle

Once upon a little while ago there lived the most
beautiful girl in the whole of the wide wide world.

She had brown eyes like almonds,
And a cute dimpled chin,
And when she smiled, the Sun smiled,
And the stars danced within.

But she was sad.

For she lived on a hill in a house that was made by a mouse
entirely out of peanut butter bricks.
It was much to the girl's dismay
That the mouse had decided to build the house this way,
As being somewhat strange,
She didn't really like peanut butter,
It wasn't for her, no way,
Not one bit,
And what's more,
She wasn't really keen on the browns and the greens which were
all that she saw,
When she looked at the hills that were outside her door,
And she would sigh and say,

"Oh gosh, what a bore,

The same every day,
I can't take any more!"

For the girl was not born to the grass and the land,
But had blood that was made up of sea salt and sand.

Yet the oceans were far from those lonely old hills,
Where time slumbered on like a snore,
And she longed, oh how she longed,
To hear waves crash and smash and splash on the shore!

"But it can't be true," little Chellington said,
"It's nothing but fluff and stuff bluffing my head!
A million, gazillion miles it seems!"

So she tried to forget it, but each night she'd dream,
Of blue waters in noonlight,
The sun on the waves,
The fingers of moonlight
In undersea caves.

But one night she stood and stared out at the sky,
And wondered if loneliness hurts when we die,
If there at the end she might finally feel whole,
Or if sadness and sorrow were part of her soul.

And she looked up at the stars and she wept and wept,
And she felt her heart break and she knew it was death,
And she beat at her chest where there was nothing left,
No joy and no happiness,
Empty
Bereft

And she screamed like a storm that turns ships to wrecks,

"Oh Gods of the Oceans,
Oh Gods of the Sea,
Take my heart as a token,
There's no love left for me!"

And she sat down and she cried and cried,
Until she could cry no more,
Picked up something shiny that lay on the floor,
When...suddenly...there came a knock at the door.

The girl who had jumped in surprise,
Got up and hastily wiping her eyes,
Opened the door to find...
...a turtle...
a turtle with a nest of hair...
Wearing cargo shorts and whose tummy was recently rather
quite fat,
But what was rather quite stranger than that,
He appeared to be reading what looked like a map.

"Hello?" said the girl.

"Oh hello," he said back, not lifting his eyes,
"Can you help me perhaps?
I've got someone to find...
...a girl...
and if you'd be so kind,

I'm looking for a house made of potato batter...is it, no wait,
never mind...
...That's not it...
...Maybe...
...Pumpkin blobber...
...Penguin biffer..."

"Peanut butter?" asked the girl.

"Peanut butter!" said the Turtle,
"My golly! That's it!
The address got all wet,
I can't read it for shit!"

And he stopped.

And for the first time he looked up at the girl,
And fell so hard in love that it stopped the whole world
From turning,
Stopped fires burning,
Winds blowing,
Rains falling,
Birds calling,
Everything...
Still...
Just still.

"So you are the girl they call Chellington Boots?
Who has coral for bones,
Tides for a pulse,
And seaweed for roots.
Tell me then, why are you here on this hill?
This place isn't yours,
These fields, they will never make you feel whole,
So I have been sent,
By the Gods of the Oceans who heard your lament,
To take you back with me, where you will be free,
To where you belong,
At home in the Sea."

"But what can this mean?" the girl said in shock,
"It's a million miles over mountains and rocks,
And fields of thorns,
And deserts and woods,
Were it possible, Turtle, it's sure that I would
Have just gone there myself such a long time ago,
But this is how things are now,
So I cannot go."

"Are you afraid?" asked the Turtle,
"Well, what is this fear?
Are you too scared to leave here because this place is near?

Or too scared to go there,
Because it's too far,
You're too scared to be what you already are,
To know what you already know,
But if you don't want to walk,
Have no worry or woe!
I'm a turtle, Chelly,
I'm famously slow,
I didn't walk here, I flew,
Much faster than sound,
Faster than light, three times round the world,
Around the moon twice,
And once more for fun,
So if you're all ready, your time here is done.
I'll take you away to the place you should be,
Where the crabs all eat cheesecake with Rooibos tea,
Where the seahorses give out their cuddles for free,
Where there are no troubles,
There's just you and me."

And Chellington Boots with no second to miss,

Dropped down to her knees,
And she gave him a kiss,
Which would have made any man dance in delight,

And he smiled and said,

"Here, hold on to me tight."

And laughing together, not one single care,
With a pop! and a hom! they were no longer there.

Chellyfish And A Blue Whale Lullaby

Fins are fun to splash around,
And flippers fun to flip,
And tails and tangly tentacles,
Are wonderful to whip.

But girls from hills look strange with gills,
And have no use for scales,

"But they sure do look beautiful,
On mermaid's brand new tails!"

So the Turtle gave his Ocean Girl the magic stuff she'd need,
And she swam about to try it out,
And looked quite fine indeed!

"How fun it is to have this tail!

And never have to breathe!
You promise I can stay down here?
I never have to leave?"

"It's not my place to promise that,
One day you'll understand,
These Seas are yours, and always were,
Now come give me your hand!
There's so many things to show you!
Things that no one's ever seen!
And places that you won't believe!
Where no girl's ever been!
But what to show you first of all to take your breath away?
The Octopus's Marathon?
The Barnacle Ballet?
The Cuttlefish's Carnival?
The Seahorses' Soiree?
But first, we must discuss the subject of your sobriquet!"

"My sobri-what?"

"Your name, my love,
This one will never do!
The one you went by up above
No longer works for you.
So let me see…
Now you're finally where you should be,
You need a name for a girl who was born to the Sea,
A name for a girl who has seaweed for roots,
For girls with no feet need no Chellington Boots…"

And the waves they were a-waving,
All the world was doing well,
All the Seas they were a-smiling,
All the Oceans feeling swell.

Little Chellyfish was laughing,
As he led her by the hand,
"So this is life!
And this is love!
At last I understand!"

"So where should we begin?
What are the sights that you must see?
What marvels should we marvel at?
To fill you up with glee?
I could show you how the Sea Squirts squirt,
When someone strokes them right,
Or how the narwhal blacksmiths forge their famous horns to
fight,
Where the penguin gets his feathers plucked,
So that he looks his best,
A proper dapper gentlemen
In tuxedo and vest.
Or what the dolphins smile about,
Why they think life's so great,
Why crabs have six legs,
Squids have ten,
And octopuses, eight,
Or..."

"Slow down!" little Chelly laughed,
"You're making my head spin!
Show me something magic!
Bowl me over like a pin!"

"I've got it! cried the Turtle,
"But it's quite a way away,
It will take a long, long time to swim!"

"Oh, Turtle, that's okay!
I'm sure that there's so much to see,
The journey will be fun!
And on the way,
We'll stop to say "Hello!" to everyone!"

And so it was they swam along,
So fast they were a blur,
And the Turtle sang her turtle songs,
And laughed along with her.

"Well, good morning!" all the creatures sang,
As they went speeding by,
"Good morning and good afternoon,
Good evening and goodbye!"

"Well, ain't she pretty?!"

"Beautiful!"

"They say she once had feet!"

"I heard that girls up on the Earth
Like crabs and fish to eat!"

And all the little children gasped!
And asked her,
"Is it true?"

"Only ones with cheese for brains!" she said.

And they said,
"Phew!
Well isn't that a big relief.
I'd hate to be a snack!"

And Chelly gave them all a kiss,
And got a thousand back!

And everywhere she went,
She made a million brand new friends,
Who came to greet her,
Shake her hand,

"My gosh it never ends!
Do the Seas go on forever?
Could I ever see them all?
The deepest ocean valleys,
And the mountains, oh so tall,
That they make the hill I come from seem like just a muddy lump,
A tiny little pile of dirt,
A teeny-tiny bump.
My gosh, it was so dreadful!"

"And you left that place behind!
That hill, that house, that hateful mouse,

They're only in your mind!
And now, my love, it's time to stop,
We have more friends to meet,
And if we're lucky they might give us something good to eat!
For every afternoon the crabs all gather here to chat,
We'll join them for a spot of tea,
And head on after that!"

"Come on, come in, sit down, that's right,
Let us pull up a seat,
Come join us for a spot of tea,
And something good to eat,
A cup of tea, for you, for me,
A biscuit for your health,
Sit down, my dear,
Most welcome here,
Tell us about yourself!"

"Most grateful, thank you,
Much obliged,
Myself?
Where to begin?
I'm just a girl called Chellyfish,
Made up of hair and skin..."

"How fascinating!
Skin and hair!
You see that we have none,
They say that you had legs before,
Which way could your legs run?

Ours just go side to side."

"Yes, mine did that as well.
But forwards, backwards, too, of course."

"And did you have a shell?"

"No, I didn't,
Sadly,
For a shell's a lovely house,
My home was on a lonely hill,
Constructed by a mouse,
Who made the bricks from peanut butter,
All the windows too,
I didn't like that place one bit,
So I decided to..."

"To what?" a little hermit asked,
And stroked her with his claw,
And Chelly touched her wrist and said,
"I was so sad before,
So lonely and so sick of all my troubles and my strife,
And so I had decided it was time to end my life..."

"Her life up there," the Turtle said,
"So she came to the Sea,
Where there's no need to think of deeds that never came to be."

And she looked at him and smiled again,
"Exactly as you say!
There is no point in looking back,
For I'm not going that way."

And the Turtle took her hand again,
"It's time for us to go,
But first I have to teach you something every girl must know,
And every little oyster child,
And every seahorse foal,
A vow we make, that if you break,
You're shunned from every shoal,
You're reviled in every rock pool,
You are snubbed in every Sea,
These words are binding,
Sacred law,
Repeat them after me:

"I make this vow upon my soul,
Upon the mighty waves,
This secret that we share,
I swear, I'll take it to my grave,
Not under any torture will our mysteries be revealed,
My will is strong,
I'll do no wrong,
My loyal lips are sealed,
And if I should digress,
If I should squeal like a bird,
If from my two-faced traitor's tongue,
Our secrets should be heard,
Then let all of the Krakens come and munch upon my head,
Let them eat my brains for breakfast,
Let them kill me til I'm dead!"

And Chelly put her hand in his,
And made the sacred vow,

And the Turtle smiled,
And kissed her hand,
And made the deepest bow,

"Now the Oceans have their Ocean Girl,
And one day she will know,
Why the Ocean Powers sent me to her
In her hour of woe.
There are ancient secrets,
Magic things,
That I must share with you,
And the greatest of them I'll reveal
Before the night is through,
But it isn't yet quite time for that,
For daylight is not done,
So let us take one more quick break,
I'll show you something fun!
There's a reef that beggars all belief,
A place of ill repute,
Where electric eels bet their volts,
In cards and craps they shoot,
Let us go and meet the worst of them,
The gamblers of the Sea,
So welcome to The Eel Casino,
Den of Misery."

"I think he's bluffing!"

"I'm not sure!"

"This is your chance to win!
I'm telling you, he ain't got nothing!
You should go all in!"

"And what do you know, Turtle?
Let me see your poker face!
You look like you are constipated!
Four kings and an ace!
I win again!"

"Wait, not so fast!
You haven't seen my hand!
You have four kings,
But I have five!
It's just as I had planned!
A hundred million volts for me,
And zero volts for you,
Oh praise the Gods!
I've beat the odds!
My lucky prayers came true!"

"You have five aces!
I have four!
How can that even be?
There's only four, and not one more,
Yet you've one more than me!
We're sick and tired of all your tricks,
Your cheating and your plots!"

And laughing, Chelly left them fighting,
Tying themselves in knots.

And they swam on together,
Turtle pulling her along,
And the Seas went on and on forever,
"I'll sing you a song!
Ahem!

One!
Two!
Ahem!
Jellyfish are smelly fish,
That I don't like one bit!
They'll sting you just for giggles,
Because they don't give a...
This is it!"

And as they stopped upon a ridge,
The Ocean girl looked down,
And couldn't hide her disappointment,
Mask her silent frown.
Down there below her was a reef,
Quite pretty, it was true,
But not the wondrous wonder he had said he'd take her to.

"It's...very nice...a lovely reef...
The nicest one I've seen...
To think that I'm the lucky one...
That no girl's ever been...
It's...wonderful...
It really is...
A striking sight for sure...
Just look at all the rocks and stuff...
I've never seen before..."

"I'm glad you like it,
I'll confess,
I think its rather bland,
But it's nice that you are so impressed,
A bonus quite unplanned.
But no, my little Chellyfish,
You'll see as they appear!
The nighttime brings them in their thousands,
Every last one here.

The greatest secret of the deep,
The Ocean Girl must know,
Is where the Blue Whales come to sleep,
In that reef down below."

And Chellyfish gasped,
And blinked her brown eyes,
For out of the watery gloom,
Ten thousand blue whales,
Whose fins were like sails,
Came into the light of the moon.

They silently settled,
And swayed in the tide,
And closed their mysterious eyes,
And to Chelly it seemed every one of their dreams
Was whispered in secretive sighs.

"I feel their snoring inside of my bones,
Like bass drums are thudding a beat,
A rhythm of wisdom,
Of rocks and of stones,
Volcanoes and fire and heat!
Such heat!
And that rhythm!
The heart of the world,

If only I still had my feet!
I see Rivers and Seas that are fires and flames,
And things being born that do not yet have names,
And Oceans in skies that are starting to drop!
Rains that won't cease!
Are refusing to stop!
How good it would feel to dance in that rain!
Just for a while to be up there again!
To feel the wind and the rain on my skin,
To dance with my love where the world will begin.
What is this I see?
Is it all in my head?"

"It's your destiny, Chelly,
The path you must tread.
But listen.
Listen.
Everything still.
Just still.
No past and no future.
No was and no will.
The Seas are yours, I swear it's so,
And one day you'll know why,
But now it's time to say goodnight,
Sweet dreams, wise whales,
Goodbye.
But there is just this one last thing,

You really have to know..."

And he whispered a secret that lit up her face,
"I cannot believe that it's so!
You swear, you're not lying?!
It isn't a joke?!"

"On the egg out of which I was born!
Every last one!"

"And all the night long?"

"From dusk,
Til they wake up at dawn."

And laughing in love,
And with tears in her eyes,
She hugged him and held him so tight,
And he kissed her and told her he'd love her forever
And took her off into the night.

So sleep mighty whales,
And dream of good stuff,
Of pizza pie plankton,
And candyfloss fluff.
Be still and be silent,
Let all worries cease,
A Blue Whale Lullaby,
Slumber in peace.

Chellyfish And The Octopuses' Marathon

Three!
Two!
One!
And the bang of a gun!
So Run! Run! Octopuses!
Run! Run! Run!

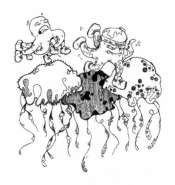

There's a race to be won!
Cheer them On! On! On!
So Run! Run! Octopuses!
Run! Run! Run!

Gotta run real fast!
Real quick!
Real brisk!
If you come in last
There's a real big risk,
That your dad will sigh,

And he'll shake his head,
And your mom will cry,
With her face all red,
And it's one more year,
Til you'll have your shot
To redeem yourself,
With a podium spot!

So Run! Run! Run! Run!
Run! Run! Run!

"It cannot be true!" Chelly frowned and said,
When she heard the talk of the racers' dread,
Of their family shame,
Of their loss of face,
How it smeared their name
Just to lose one race.

"Do they care so much?
It's the strangest thing!"

"It's a mighty prize!
All his life,
He's king!
He's the Ocean Champ!
Creatures near and far,
Come to cheer and stamp,
He's an eight point star!"

"All his life, he's king?!
Tell me, why not queen?!"

"Don't get mad with me,
But there's just not been,
Any girl that's won,
Or has even tried,
It's a risky run,

Many boys have died,
It's no friendly jog,
It is wild and rough,
There are tricks and traps,
Real ambush stuff."

"And a girl's too weak?
Well, I guess we'll see!
Because look!
That looks like a girl to me!"

And to the crowd's delight,
And the Turtle's shock,
A little octopus,
At the starting blocks,
Puffed her cute cheeks out,
Checked her bow was straight,

And her opponents laughed!

"It is not too late!"

And she looked around with her big brown eyes,
At those mean old brutes,
Who were twice her size.

"You can still back out!
Run off home instead!

For there is no doubt,
You will end up dead!"

And she blushed and blinked,
Gave a nervous smile,
And then from her mouth,
Came a vow so vile!
Came a curse so crude!
Came an oath so bad!
All the parents there,
All the moms and dads,
With their fins and feet,
Covered children's ears!

Crying,
"Don't repeat any words you hear!"

But the children laughed,
And they swore and swore,

"You're a lobster's sack!
You're a crab's backdoor!"

Chelly laughed and laughed,
And she caught her eye,
Shouted,

"Best of luck!
Show them all!
Don't die!"

And the girl smiled back,

"It is time we won!"

And a
Three!
Two!

One!
And the bang of a gun!
So Run! Run! Octopuses!
Run! Run! Run!
Run! Run! Run!
Run! Run!
Run! Run! Run!

Now the Octopuses' Marathon
Is quite the magic race.
And for a magic race so magical
You need a magic place,
And the magicalest place of all is in the Rainbow Reef,
Where the colors of the coral cause a sigh of disbelief!
There are reds and flaming oranges,
And polyps, pink and blue,
Purples, greens and indigoes,
And brightest yellows too.
There are waterfalls,
That grey old men will tell you can't exist,
But the magic worlds of magic girls don't care for scientists.
So along with mighty waterfalls,
Volcanoes, six feet high,
That blow out bubbles,
Big as blimps,
And small as tadpoles eyes.
There are great big rocks,
In seaweed socks,
With pompoms on their toes,
And monkey mice,
All sniffing rice and seasalt up their nose.
There are ocean flowers,
That dance and sing,
And cactuses that scat,
And trees that sneeze
Whose snots are cheese,

Exploding with a splat.
And loads of other magic stuff
Just take me at my word
A perplexing place of wonder
With a pinch of the absurd.

But looks can be deceiving
Pretty smiles hide hungry teeth,
And for all its bonkers beauty,
There lurked danger in the reef.
There were holes and spikes,
And drops and dykes,
Unseen at such a pace,
And as no-one stopped,
Would sooner drop down dead than lose the race,
Every year they fell,
A shiny hell,
But still the runners came,
For to take first place,
That deadly race,
Brought fortune,
Fans and Fame.

For the octopus who could keep his nerve,
Didn't tumble,
Trip,
Who could stand and swerve,
Miss the spikiest spikes,
Round the tightest curves,
Who just laughed at death,
With vivacious verve,
All the Seas were his,
Til his days were done,
When he crossed the line,
When the race was won,
All his dreams came true,

He got everything,
What a mighty prize!
All his life,
A king!
Hail the Ocean champ!
Creatures near and far,
Come to cheer and stamp,
For the eight point star!

So Run! Run! Octopuses!
Run! Run! Run!

Run! Run! Run!
Run! Run!
Run! Run! Run!

Run! Run! Run! Ru...

Run?

Run!

Why don't they run?

They're all piled up,
All tangled,
Except for that one!

And she ran with her tentacles all but a blur!

"Their shoes are all tied up!
It must have been her!"

And she looked back and laughed at the chaotic scene,

"I'm tired of Kings!
This whole thing is obscene!"

And she ran and she ran!
And she ran and she ran!
And she ran and she ran and she ran and she ran!

And she ran and she ran and she ran and she ran!

But her legs couldn't grow anymore than yours can,
And the racers, untangled and started to run!
And started to catch up!

But not every one!

There were some on the ground!
What grunts and what groans!
The dreadfulest sounds!
All curses and moans!

For it wasn't just she who had laid out her traps,
For the winner was never the fastest of laps,
The hardest of trainers,
Who'd memorized maps,
Had planned out their route,
And avoided mishaps,
It was vicious and violent,
As Turtle had said,
And to run was a risk
Where you risked being dead.

So the weakest fell first,
Or the ones who were kind,
Who slowed down to help them and fell far behind,
Then the ones who were honest,
Who ran by the rules,
For despite what your teachers might tell you in school,
As sad it is,
Crime is certain to pay,
And cheaters do prosper,
The rich get their way,
Who cheat more than anyone,
Make up the law,
To steal what is left from the mouths of the poor,
Compassionless free-for-all,
Power and wealth,
An Octopus Marathon,
Each for himself.

But the cute, little Octopus,
Had no such greed,
Was as pure as can be in both thought and in deed,
She ran for a cause,
That was righteous and true,
She ran for the many who starved for the few,
She ran for the sick who were too weak to run,
She ran for the homeless whose value was none,

She ran for the old who'd been left in the past,
She ran for the masses who'd always come last,

"My gods how I hate it!
This way that we live!
Where the losers in life are the ones who forgive,
Are the neighbourly souls,
On whose shoulders you lean,
And the winners are those who are heartless and mean,
Who see kindness as softness,
And fairness as weak,
Who step on the throats of the mild and the meek!
I will beat them all at it!
I'll win their damn race!
I'll shame every one of them!
All in disgrace!
And not one will come again,
Not one will dare!
We'll make a new race,
A new world that is fair."

And she ran and she ran though her legs screamed to stop!
Swerved around corners
And skipped across drops!
Bounced across jellyfish,
Slipped on their slime,
But as hard as she ran she knew all of the time,
They were catching her up,
They were right on her tail,
She could see them all sneering and hoping she'd fail,
Hear all their vitriole,
Feel their hate,
But suddenly where there were once only eight,
She had 63 legs!
And there was one more!
And she sped along eight times more fast than before,

"My gods what has happened?
I've so many feet!
And every last one of them ever so fleet!
And ever so nimble!
And ever so light!
But I have no control of them!
Try as I might!"

And she shot on like lightning!
She flew like a flash!

"They've got minds of their own!
I am certain to crash!"

But her new magic legs never stumbled or slipped,
Never tangled or twisted up,
Tumbled or tripped,
They carried her on,
Although she had no say,

"What spell am I under?
Who made me this way?"

And there was the finish line!
Just round that bend!
And then at that moment approaching the end,
Her legs all divided,
One eighth of before,
And she crossed the line,
Laughing,
And heard the crowd roar!

And Chelly was cheering,
And all were in tears,
The first girl who'd won in a billion years,
And they gathered around her and hoisted her up,
And held out the ancient most magical cup,
The Rainbow Reef Trophy,
The number one prize,
But the girl wouldn't take it,
To shock and surprise,

"I don't want your trophy,
I don't want your cheers,
This race for millennia,
Millions of years,
Has caused so much misery,
Sorrow and pain,
The meanest ones winning again and again,
Well look at them now!
I have beaten them all!
A cute little octopus 12 inches tall,
We don't need to race,
It's the stupidest thing!
No need for a winner!
A queen or a king!"

And all of the runners,
All sulking, in shame,
All shuffled off, skulking,
And cursing her name,
And that was the end of the Rainbow Reef Race.
For no-one thereafter would risk such disgrace,
And when any octopus acted unkind,
One look from that girl was enough to remind,
The Oceans were changing,
The new world was fair,
And all who looked backwards had better beware.

And the Ocean Girl gave her a hug and a kiss.

"I know it was you I must thank for all this.
Your magical legs took me over the line,
The victory's yours,
Even more that it's mine."

But Chellyfish frowned,

"I don't know what you mean."

"Not you?
Well then whose could the magic have been?"

And watching it all with the ghost of a grin,
That showed all his teeth that were sharp as his fin,
A shark in the shadows who'd watched the girl run
Who'd tore down injustice the moment she'd won,
Shook his head gently,

"It's only the start,
So much inequality tears us apart."

And he gritted his teeth,
And he spoke to the night,

"Give me half her strength,
When it's my turn to fight."

And with a swish of his dorsal,
That stranger was gone,
Who had given her legs that had carried her on.

But Magical legs only take you so far,
What courage!
What heart!
Little eight-pointed star!

So run though you know there's no way you will win,
Finish for those without strength to begin,
And if you come last, or you come in first place,
Know life's an adventure,
There's no need to race.

Three Little Fish And A
Turtle Called Elvis

Pennyfish and Willowfish and Lilyfish were silly fish,
Were real silly billy fish,
Just playing willy-nilly fish,
Who caused all mire and mischief for the Turtle and for
Chellyfish,
And teased the sharks and jellyfish,
And called them farts and smelly fish.

Who on this boring morning, yawning,
Tried to think up stuff to do,
Some prank, or jinx or bluff or two,
Just something not to feel so blue.

But had no ideas left for ways to trick the other ocean folk,
Were all tricked out,
Their brains all broke,

Until their leader Penny spoke,

"Come on, I'm getting restless,
What a hopeless waste of vital time,
We need to go incite some crime,
So rack your brains, now, friends of mine.
Use all your mental pots and pans,
To cook up sneaky plots and plans.
Just think now, Willow!
Lily think!
How we can cause the biggest stink!
Use all your minds, the kitchen sink!
What trouble can we make for fun?
Jog your memories, make them run!
Of all the naughty things we've done."

"But Penny," little Lilly said,
"There's someone not accounted for,
Whose foiled us many times before,
The scruffy haired cantankerous bore,
Who moans and groans about the law,
Who lectures til we start to snore!"

"Now listen, girls!" said Willow standing up, looking all stern and
gruff,
"Let's cut out all this silly stuff!
I'm telling you I've had enough.
I don't have time to chase you round the whatsit and the blah
blah blah!
No! This time you have gone too far!"

"That's just like, Turtle! Ha! Ha! Ha!"

"He's really such a bozo,
And so soppy that I want to spew!
Just barf my brains up!"

"That's so true!"

"He really doesn't have a clue!"

"The only thing he talks about is Chellyfish."

"It's really sad."

"...Oh, all the magic times we've had..."

"He's duller even than my dad!"

"...You see, girls, she was on this hill..."

"...I had this map..."

"...and still.."

"...just still..."

"I spied on him just yesterday,
My Gods!
The things I overheard!
He's wrote a poem!"

"That's absurd!"

"I heard him practice,
Word for word."

"The Turtle cannot write a poem,
He can barely wipe his bum."

"His brains are cheese and bubblegum!"

"I heard it and it's really dumb,
'If Chelly was a caterpillar she would be the best,
She would have the cutest horns and be more hairy than the rest,
And if Chelly was a chicken she would lay the biggest eggs,
I would eat them all for breakfast, then her wings and then her legs,
And if Chelly was a monkey she would throw the furthest poo,

She would throw it half a mile more than other monkeys do,
And if Chelly was a kangaroo she'd have the highest jump,
She would box the other kangaroos, give them a well hard thump,
And if Chelly was a penguin…"

"You must stop before you make me sick!"

"How can he think that he's so slick?"

"Does Chellyfish not know he's thick?"

"I've often wondered that myself,
I guess she must be dumb as well."

"Her head's as hard as Turtle's shell."

"Their brains just share a single cell."

"Remember, girls, when Turtle warned us Chellyfish had scary
eyes?
And everyone was all surprised?
And when she'd come we'd run and hide?"

"Because he said the Sirens were all really nice she got all mad!"

"But I don't see why that was bad?"

"Me neither, so I asked my dad."

"He started mumbling nonsense,
Started bumbling, sweating, went all red.
I couldn't hear a word he said."

"Perhaps he thought he'd end up dead?
That Chellyfish would come and that her
eyes would chop him into bits!"

"You know I think that must be it.
Cos he was frightened out his wits!
I told him I would ask my mom and he
looked like he'd seen a ghost!"

"He must have thought that he was toast!"

"She'd put him in a pot to roast!"

"I heard the strangest thing from Chelly,
Something that just can't be true!
That's so superb!…it can't be true!"

"What is it?!"

"There's no way it's true!"

"Tell us!"

"Gods, let it be true!"

"Lily, we are begging you!"

"The other day when I was helping Chelly fix her garden up,
Just cleaning, preening, boring stuff,
Like real day-dreaming, snoring stuff,
From nothing Chelly asked me if I'd ever seen a sleeping whale,
That Turtle told her quite a tale…"

"That scruffy Giant Ocean Snail!
We have no time to hear another Turtle tale,
They're never fun!"

"But listen! Wait, until I'm done!
This isn't like his usual ones.

He might be dull but Turtle knows about all kinds of secret stuff,
Like classified and covert stuff,
Like sensitive and spying stuff."

"Like sneaky ocean ninja stuff?"

"Like dark and dangerous monster stuff?"

"Exactly! Not his usual fluff!
Well, he has sworn to all the Gods that he will not reveal a thing!
An on his honour kind of thing,
But he tells Chelly everything!
The greatest secret of the Sea
Is where the mighty blue whales sleep,
Their giant beds beneath the deep,
Where they all snooze and count their sheep!"

"And Chelly told you where it was?
Oh Gods! We have to go and see!"

"And hear them snore!"

"Like giants roar!"

"But wait, there's more!
Come close to me!"

And little Lily dropped her voice, and whispered like a tiny bird,
So that she was not overheard,
No prying ears could catch a word,

"The Turtle said that whales have to take a super giant breath,
Before they sink down to the depths,
Or else they'll die a sleepy death,
But here's the thing, when stuff is full of air it always starts to
bloat,
And all that air will make it float,
Imagine giant whale boats,

The humans would all come along and pluck them out like,

"One, two, three!"

"A whale for you! A whale for me!"

"They'd use their bones to drink their tea!"

"So whales have this special trick that keeps them on the ocean bed,
And stops them floating off instead,
So humans can't chop off their heads,
Or spread their brains on toasted bread.
That stops them ending up all dead.
They swim down to the bottom, close their eyes, and when their dreaming starts,
They start to let out tiny farts,
Meticulously spaced apart.
But think now girls, what if that gas was all released at just one time?
An instantaneous bottom chime!
A work of art, a farty rhyme!
Let's go and see the whales and we will sneak in there without a peep,
And find a baby sleeping deep
That's all tucked up and sound asleep,
Is dreaming sweetly, brewing up a monumental mighty gas,
And there will be a frightful blast,
A great explosion from its ass,
If we could wake it with a shock,
So that it loses all control!"

"A mighty bang of rock and roll!"

"Explodes out of its bottom hole!"

"The whales won't be there yet,
But to get there it will take all day!"

"Let's set off now!"

"Yes! No delay!"

"Come on then, girls, I know the way!"

And with their eyes a-gleaming,
Brains a-scheming,
They were speeding off,
To make the whales' bottoms cough,
To blow their bloated backsides off,
But swimming there behind them
Always hiding, staying out of sight,
A shadow in the morning light,
Who'd heard them cackle in delight,
Who followed them until the sunlit waters turned to inky black,
Who had a shell upon his back,
Snuck up as they planned their attack.

"Look at that little baby there,
His bottom's bigger than the moon!"

"His bum will make the biggest boom!"

"Stand back now, girls, give me some room,
Yes, that's the one, he's perfect,
Roll the rock up right here to the edge,
We'll drop it on him from this ledge,
Before we do let's make the pledge,
Let's cross our hearts,
And make a solemn oath that we will never tell,
And if we do we'll go to hell!
The hottest bit of it as well!"

"I make this vow upon my soul,
Upon the mighty waves,
This secret that we share,
I swear, I'll take it to my grave,

Not under any torture will our mysteries be revealed,
My will is strong,
I'll do no wrong,
My loyal lips are sealed,
And if I should digress,
If I should squeal like a bird,
If from my two-faced traitor's tongue,
Our secrets should be heard,
Then let all of the Krakens come and munch upon my head,
Let them eat my brains for breakfast,
Let them kill me til I'm dead!"

"What if it makes a tidal wave a billion, zillion miles high?
Or blows the Seas into the sky?
Then everyone we know will die."

"I think it's just a risk that we will have to take."

"I must agree."

"A stinky Sea catastrophe."

"It's worth it."

"Okay, count to three!"

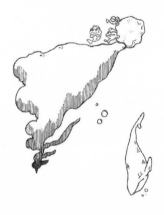

"We'll drop the rock right on his head, and
cross our fins and tails too."

"Let's hope the shock don't make him poo."

"Okay, girls, ready,
One!
Aaaaaaaaaand
Two!
Aaaaaaaand…!"

"Stop!" a little voice cried out,
A tiny little nervous sound,
The naughty fish all spun around,
And can you guess who they all found?

"Elvis!" they cried out at once,
"How did you know where we would be?"

"Get out of here just leave us be."

"There's nothing here for you to see!"

"It's naughty!" little Elvis said, peeping his head out of his shell.

"Imagine what a monstrous smell!"

"You're all so bad! I'm going to tell!"

"You traitor!" little Lily said,
"You always tell! It isn't kind!"

"That's why you're always left behind!"

"And have no friends!"

"Well, I don't mind…
I'd rather have no friends than always be told off for being bad."

But inside he was feeling sad,
And missed the friends he'd never had.

"Come on, it's time to go,
Or I will tell the Turtle what you've done."

"You're just like him, the foe of fun!"

"And that's why there's not anyone who
ever wants to play with you!"

"Because you're such a tattle-tale!"

"It's just a stupid stinky whale!"

"It's fart will break the Richter Scale!"

"It's naughty!" Elvis shouted back,
And jumped upon the giant rock,
"What if the whale dies from shock?
Awoken with a cinder block!"

"Ummm, Elvis...." little Lily said,

"A boulder dropped upon his bed!
What if the whale wakes up dead?
The gas explodes inside his head?"

"But Elvis...!"

"It is time to go!"

"But Elvis...!!!!!"

"I don't want to know!
Pack up your fins!"

"But Elvis!"

"No!
I do not care!
I swear you're soooooooOOOOOOOOO-
OOOOOOOOOOOOOOO...!"

The little fish rushed to the edge and watched the boulder tumble
off,
The timid turtle crying,
"Stop!"
And helplessly, they saw it drop,
And watched it sink with little Elvis holding on with all his
might,
Behind his glasses, eyes shut tight,
When with a fearful fearsome fright,
The baby whale was woken when the rock was bounced right off
its head,
But unlike little Elvis said,
It did not wake up one bit dead.
It woke up angry,
Super mad,
Bonkers,
Barmy,
Big time bad,
Thrashing,
Splashing,
Full of rage,
Murderous and half deranged,
And Lily, Willow and their leader Penny watched in silent awe,
Were shell-shocked by its raging roar!
A sound like nothing heard before.

That rumbled like a tidal bore,
That rippled through the ocean floor,
And all the whales started stirring,
Stretching fins,
And blinking eyes,
And stared around in stern surprise,
And heard the baby's booming cries,
And woken from their snoring,
Not yet morning!
All the whales rose,
Were roaring oaths of violent blows,

"WHO INTERRUPTS OUR PEACEFUL DOZE?!"

And looked up at the little fish all frozen still in frightened shock,
And looked down at the giant rock,
That like some evil cuckoo clock,
Had woken them from happy dreams of candied
krill and plankton pies,

"OUR SLUMBERS HAVE BEEN VANDALISED!
OUR PEACEFUL TRANCES TERRORISED!"

When to the fishes' great surprise,
They saw with most astounded eyes,

That there was little Elvis,
Just a puny blob of frightened green,
A microscopic lima bean,
Who until now had not been seen,
Was struggling, squirming, stuck securely in the whale's
breathing hole,

A tiny Elvis sausage roll,
Whose terror touched his turtle soul,
Who watched in silent pleading as the little fish all backed away,
All turned their tails and swam away,
And swam til they were far away!

And when the dark succumbed to light,
The morning shooed away the night,
The blackness scuttled off in fright,
The gloominess becoming bright,

The little fish, stopped swimming,
And went up to watch the new Sun rise,
Were barely holding back their cries,
Could barely meet each other's eyes,

"Elvis..." little Lily said,
Her eyes betraying a single tear,
Her tiny heart filled up with fear,

But Penny didn't want to hear,

"We cannot think of that right now,
We have to make up some excuse,
That's so complex,
That's so obtuse..."

"What if he's turned to Elvis Juice...?!
Or squished up into Elvis Mousse...?!"

"We'll try to tell the Turtle that we're sorry for our silliness,
Repentant, full of willingness,
Be good 'til he's forgiven us."

"But Willow, will he listen?
It's the same old thing we always say,
Remember just the other day,
We threw his favourite shells away."

""I can't believe what you have done!
It boggles me you'd even dare!
Now what am I supposed to wear?
Just cargo shorts and scruffy hair?!""

"Let's go and plead with Chellyfish and tell her that we messed up
bad,
Our naughtiness is just a fad,
The Turtle might not be so mad."

"If Chellyfish talks to him he'll get soppy like he always does..."

"...he won't cause such a needless fuss..."

"...or shout or swear or curse or cuss..."

"...or swell or yell or lecture us..."

"But Elvis..." little Lily said,
And all their faces turned to red,

"We can't just leave him there for dead
No matter what the whales said!
We need a plan that much is clear,
To save him from that stinky lump,
Some way to give it some hard thump,
Or kick it up it's slimy rump!
To...help our friend."

And Lily sniffed,
And tears ran down her little face,

"We left him in that dreadful place
Who cares about our own disgrace?
I bet he's scared!"

And none of them could look into each others' eyes,

"Because of us, of all our lies!"

"Now what if little Elvis dies?!"

"You're right," said Penny, looking stern,
"I'm sorry,
I was so afraid,
We must clean up this mess we've made,
Now's not the time to be dismayed.
I've got a plan,
So gather round,
It isn't for the faint of heart,
It's likely we'll be ripped apart,
And baked into a hake-filled tart,
Whales are strong and big
But what's the thing that all the Ocean fears?,
Whose eyes are fire,
Whose teeth are spears,
Has slept now for a thousand years!"

"You're joking?!"

"There's no other way,
The first three fish to ever dare,
Were brave and bold!
Would not beware!
Who went down to the Kraken's lair."

Here follows now a story Ocean moms and dads tell girls and
boys,
To scare them when there's too much noise,

And so they'll clean up ocean toys,
A story of a beast that every fisherman and sailor dreads,
That gives them nightmares in their beds,
Of monsters munching off their heads.

A story every child knows up on the land and in the sea,
So if you're sitting comfortably,
Let me begin in...

One

Two

Three

'When all the Seas were made,
Although by what or whom was not agreed,
Well, everything was fine indeed,
And all had all that all could need,
And all the Oceans got along,
And all were friends and all were fine,
What's mine is yours,
What's yours is mine,
'Til suddenly a fishing line,
The very first was cast out by a greedy man who fancied fish,
Sashimi or a dolphin dish,
Who dropped his line and made a wish...

"I wish the Gods would send to me a mighty meal to fill me up,
So giant it would be enough
To stuff me til I'm really stuffed,
Til I am bursting out my seams,
Til seafood fills my sleepy dreams,
To bloat me like a big balloon on giant crabs or bulging breams."

So kind and good, the Ocean Gods were pleased to grant the man's
request,
The Seas politely acquiesced,

And sent the biggest and the best,
The most delicious, most colossal creature in the Seven Seas,
Who like the Gods was keen to please,
But when the man reeled in his hook he fell in fear down to his
knees,
And begged the Gods to
"Take it back!
Forgive my pleas for Ocean snacks!
My eyes were blind with greed,
Indeed there is no need for this attack!
Don't eat me!"

And the creature smiled,
"You wanted meat that's not so wild?
A friendly little flounder,
Or some chubby, cheerful mermaid child?"

And then it took a giant Gulp!
And chewed the man up into pulp!
A squelchy, squirmy human pulp!
A chewy, gooey person pulp!

Then back off to its hole it skulked…

And waited there in hungry sleep,
Until the time to feed again,
A man or woman, fine or plain,
A Pie of Steve or Quiche Lorraine.'

And now into that horrid hole,
With plucky hearts, our heroes came,
Whose little souls were full of shame,

"If Elvis dies, we'll be to blame!"

They whispered, swimming slowly, bravely,
Down into the murky gloom,
Into the Kraken's sleepy tomb,

"We'll save him from his whaley doom!"

"We have to!
If the whales squish him he'll be such an awful sulk!"

"Look at this great, big heaving bulk!"

"WHO DARES TO WAKE THE OCEAN HULK?!
WHO DARES TO SNEAK DOWN TO MY LAIR,
WHISPERING LIKE LITTLE SPIES?!
ASSASSIN FISHES IN DISGUISE?!
WHO'VE COME TO TAKE ME BY SURPRISE?!"

And quite rudely awoken,
These words spoken through its razor teeth,
The kraken laughed in disbelief,

"SUCH PUNY PIRATES!
TINY THIEVES!"

And swearing oaths of murder, pledging broken bones and
munched off heads,
The Kraken rose from out its bed,
With twenty eyes all flashing red,
A thousand teeth all razor sharp,
And tentacles like slithering snakes,

"I'LL SMASH YOU INTO SALMON SHAKES!
I'LL HAMMER YOU TO HADDOCK CAKES!"

"We are not thieves or pirates!" little Lily said,
"And we don't sneak!
We've come here 'cos we need to speak,
We need your help…"

"..for we're so weak,
And you're so strong, and mighty…"

"Such a noble beast, there's never been!"

"The mightiest monster ever seen!"

"A face to grace the silver screen!"

"Indeed, that's right," said Willow,
"Looks that kill!"

"Oh, what a dazzling smile!"

"Those yellow teeth are so in style!"

"Those tentacles so versatile!"

"And all your eyes…!"

"THAT'S QUITE ENOUGH!
WHAT IS IT THAT YOU CAME TO SAY?!
MAKE SURE IT DOESN'T TAKE ALL DAY!
JUST SPIT IT OUT, THEN ON YOUR WAY!"

"We need your help!"
And they explained…

"…a secret Chelly couldn't keep…"

"…and when the whales go to sleep…"

"…they have to stay down in the deep.."

"…with tiny farts…"

"…imagine that…!"

"…and so we snuck up late last night…"

"…the baby whale had quite the fright…"

"…but Elvis…"

"…stuck…"

"…it serves him right…"

"…he really shouldn't always tell…"

"Penelope!"

"Okay!"

"…so, well, that's why we're here…"

"…to ask for aid…"

"…to help us fix the mess we've made…"

"…we left our friend in trouble…"

"…farty bubbles…"

"…must be so afraid…"

"Please help us!"

And the little fish,
All held their fins in pleading prayer,

"Take pity on us!"

"Our despair!"

"Please come and give the whales a scare!"

"And we can get our friend back!"

"He'll be safe and sound!"

"And we'll repent!"

"...that is to say..."

"...what Lily meant..."

"I've made quite clear my intent!
We'll change our ways for good this time,
We'll make amends,
I swear it's true!
Our castigation's overdue.
Please help us now!
We're begging you!"

And that great sprawling, spiteful beast
Looked down upon her pleading face,
A flower in that frightful place,
Whose tears of shame had left their trace,
Their marks upon her little cheeks,
Which glowed with wrath and youthful grit,
And did not fear the beast one bit,
Whose eyes spat flames like dragon spit,
And its great black and hateful heart was softened by her reckless
will,
Her looks that looked like looks could kill,
It smiled and said,

"A SLEEPING PILL."

"A sleeping what?" the Three Fish asked.

"A PILL THAT MAKES THEM COUNT THEIR SHEEP,
TO KEEP THOSE VIOLENT WHALES ASLEEP.
SO THERE AMONGST THEM YOU CAN CREEP,
CAN SKULK LIKE LITTLE PIRATES DO,
LIKE LITTLE THIEVES,

TO FIND YOUR FRIEND,
AND WHEN YOU DO I'D RECOMMEND,
YOU SNEAK ROUND TO THE WHALE'S BACKEND,
AND PLUG IT UP WITH SOMETHING STRONG,
SOME SEAWEED THAT IT CAN'T EXPEL,
AND HOPE THAT IT ALL TURNS OUT WELL,
BUT IF THE WHALE STARTS TO SWELL,
YOU'D BETTER SWIM...!"

And with a wink, the kraken turned its ancient head,

"NOW LEAVE ME BE,
I'M GOING TO BED,
IF YOU COME BACK I'LL MUNCH YOUR HEADS."

And whispering words of thankfulness,
They swam back out in disbelief,
With beaming smiles of wild relief,
And raced off to the Whales' Reef.

"A sleeping pill," said Willow,
Looking down upon the dozing crowd,
Already snoozing, snoring loud,
And farting booming mushroom clouds,

"To keep them sleeping," Penny said,
"To make sure that their eyes are shut,
So in amongst them, we can strut,
Shove seaweed up that baby's..."

"But...
What on earth's a sleeping pill?
It sounds to me like human stuff."

"Like dry-land nonsense."

"Up-there fluff."

"Think out the box, girls!
Off the cuff!
We'll improvise!
That's what we do!
We've played ten thousand pranks before!
And after those, ten thousand more!
So think!
That's what we're famous for!"

"I cannot think," said Lily,
"When I try, I'm haunted by his face!
His scruffy hair and puffed-up face!
His stupid, pompous stuck-up face!
The Turtle!"

And as one they groaned,

"He'll lecture us until we die!"

"Until our ears begin to cry!"

"Until we kiss our brains goodbye!"

"Until he puts us all to sleep!"

"Enchants us all with earache!"

"A sleep from which we can't awake!"

"A trance!"

"A spell that none can break!"

"A lecture..."

"...that's so boring..."

"...we'll be snoring..."

And as one they stopped!

And in their brains, the same plan popped!
For all at once, the penny dropped!

And Willow stood up on the cliff,
And looking down all stern and gruff,
Said,
"Cut out all this silly stuff!
I'm telling you, I've had enough!
We don't have time to sneak around your big backsides and angry
tails!
You're such a bunch of stinky whales!
Your disrespect is off the scales!
Your naughtiness…"

And as she droned,
Her little friends snuck through the horde,
Whose snores and farts were booming chords,

When Lily yawned,
"My Gods, I'm bored!"

"The lecture, Lily!
Be real quick!"
And plug your little ears up tight!
Quick, take this seaweed!"

"Gosh, you're right!
It's so humdrum, it's hard to fight!"

And stuffing seaweed in their ears,
They saw the whale they'd come to find,
And snuck up on it from behind,
For bottom holes are mostly blind,
And there was Elvis,
Half asleep,

"He's looking rather sickly grey."

"He has been stuck since yesterday."

"Lets plug him up, now,
No delay!"

And with this rather stinky task completed,
They retreated fast,
Afraid there'd be a frightful blast,
A great explosion from its ass,
But while the whale didn't stir,
And did not open sleeping eyes,
It silently began to rise,
The fish all gasping in surprise,

"Whales have this special trick that keeps them on the ocean bed,
And stops them floating off instead,
So humans can't chop off their heads!"

"Or spread their brains on toasted bread!"

"That stops them ending up all dead!"

They swim down to the bottom, close their eyes,
and when their dreaming starts…"

"They start to let out tiny farts!"

"Meticulously spaced apart!"

And as the baby whale breached the cold night air,
It blinked its eyes,
It saw the moonlit, starry skies,
"What are these flaming fireflies?!"

And as it blew its hole in joy, it saw a tiny shooting star,
But one that looked a bit bizarre,

"Oh great! He's blown him really far!"
"Come back here, Elvis!" they all cried,

But Elvis could not hear a word,
Was flying higher than a bird,
And while this might sound quite absurd,
He laughed as he was flying,
No denying, he was really scared,
For landing, he was unprepared,
His limbs, he hoped, could be repaired,
But they had come to save him,
And it filled his heart with happy smiles,
Whilst rocketing for miles and miles,
For in the littlest of whiles...

He'd see his friends again.

Chellyfish And The King Of Sharks

There was a deep dark cave,
In the deep blue sea,
That was a very, very, very, very,
very, very, very, very,
scary, scary, scary, very scary place to be.

For in that deep dark cave,
In the deep blue sea,
That was a very, very, very, very,
very, very, very, very,
scary, scary, scary, very scary place to be,
In the place most deep,
In the place most dark,
Lived the great big King of the Great White Sharks.

For a thousand years he'd been a mean old thing,
With a mean old mouth,
And a mean old grin,
With a million teeth,
And with scarred up skin,

And a scarred up eye,
And a scarred up fin,
That was ten feet tall,
And was midnight black,
That was like a crown on the old King's back.

To ascend the throne of the Great White Sharks,
Is no piece of cake for the faint of hearts,
For the Shark King's crown isn't easy won,
It is not passed down to the old king's son.

You must seize the right!
Call the old king out!
To the death you fight!
Rip his old gills out!
Smash his old skull in!
Chew his old eyes out!
Tear his old fins off!
Spill his insides out!

Let the Oceans know,
Let them cower in fear!
For a new time's come,
And a new king's here!
And the sharks all bow,
And you take your seat,
On the throne of bones,
It is time to eat!

Little children's hands,
Little children's feet,
Little children's blood,
Are a tasty treat!

Gulp it all down neat!
Little children's bones,
Little children's meat,

Little children's heads,
Are a meal most sweet.

Yum! Yum! Yummy! Yummy!
Yum!
Yum!
Yum!

For the only food,
For a king so wild,
Is the tender meat of a human child.

So listen, little children who go swimming in the sea,
You should know that ocean waters are a hairy place to be,
There are dangerous tides,
And spikes that hide,
And tiny holes with things inside,
That bite your feet or nip your toes,
Will scrape your knees and bite your nose,
But worse than spikes,
Or stuff that stings,
Are the mean old sharks of the mean old King,
All the stinking sharks of the mean old King!
All the odorous sharks Of the mean old King!

Who every day go scavenging for yummy little kids,
For tasty little Bills and Bettys,
Susans, Seans and Sids,
Delicious little Daves and Daisys,
Kevins, Karls and Kims,

Scrummy little Toms and Taylors,
Judys, Johns and Jims,
To take back to their mean old ruler,
Offer with a bow,

"Here, sire, I've brought you breakfast,
Please enjoy your chow!"

But sharks are the dumbest creatures in the Seven Seas,
Their brains are made of snot and stuff that shoot out when you
sneeze,
They don't count past five,
When the number's ten,
They just count to five,
Then they start again,
When they try to spel,
They giv up and gess,
They will answer "no",
When the answer's "yes",
When the test is hard,
They will try to cheat,
Or write naughty words on their answer sheet.

Like "LOBSTER SACKS!"
And "SEASNAKE FEET!"
Like "CRABS' BACKDOORS!"
And "MERMAID MEAT!"

So here is the first lesson every mom and dad should teach,
Whenever you go swimming, kids,
Don't stray far from the beach!

For a shark is fast,
But its brain is bad,
So you must make sure
You can see your dad,
Tell him where you'll swim,

Keep your mom in sight,
For a shark's no match,
In a no rules fight,
With a murderous mom,
A demented dad,
Who will kick its bum,
'Til it swims off sad,
To the deep dark cave,
In the deep blue sea,
That's a very, very, very, very,
Very, very, very, very,
Scary, scary, scary, very scary place to be,
And he'll tell the king,
That the child was smart,
Didn't come too deep,
Didn't stray too far,
And the shark will weep,
And he'll kneel and scrape,
But his mournful pleas will come far too late,
And he'll make his peace,
And he'll bow his head,
And the King of Sharks
Eats him up instead.

Yuck! Yuck! Yucky! Yucky!
Yuck!
Yuck!
Yuck!

Now the littlest while after Chelly first came to the Sea,
To that cave that was so dark and such a scary place to be,
There came a shark who'd never once been to that place before,
Who had never once paid homage,
Never knelt upon the floor,
Who had never sworn allegiance,
Never made a loyal vow,

Who had never come and made an oath,
Had never come to bow,
But he came now, smiling, all alone,
And here is what he said,

"I've come to take the Shark King's Throne,
It's time that you were dead."

And the mean old Shark King laughed and laughed,
And laughed until he cried,

"This pipsqueak comes to challenge?
Has his skull no brains inside?
Just swim away now little fish,
You don't want to get hurt,
I could eat you whole and still have room for starter and dessert!"

And the new shark smiled,
But he did not speak,
He just waited
Still
Didn't make a squeak
And the old king roared,
And he gnashed in rage,

"I have been the king,
For an Ocean Age!
Every one who tried!
I have slaughtered them!
You're the thousandth one!
Come and die now then!"

And the young shark braced for the king's attack,
And he watched him come,
And his mind went back,
To a hateful race,
And to one so bold,

She had shocked the Seas,
Though a few years old,
And had won that race,
Little eight point girl,
Who had changed the face of the Ocean world.

And he smiled again,

"Now my time has come!
She gave me heart to fight,
I gave her legs to run!
One day we'll fight together,
But now I stand alone,
I will kill this King
And I will take his throne!
I will seize the right!
Call the old king out!
To the death we'll fight!
I'll rip his old gills out!
Smash his old skull in!
Chew his old eyes out!
Tear his old fins off!
Spill his insides out!"

And they fought and fought,

Til the seas were red,
And the new Shark King,
Left the old King dead,
And he took his crown,
Sat in his great seat,
On the throne of bones,
It was time to eat.

Yuck! Yuck! Yucky! Yucky!
Yuck! Yuck! Yuck!

And all the most ambitious creatures heard of this new King,
And scratched their greedy heads to think what bribe was best to
bring,
How to gain his royal favour,
How to use it for their ends,
How to use his power to grow their own,
And rise above their friends.

But this new Shark King was not one bit
like those who'd come before.

"I have no time for sycophants who scrape upon my floor.
For there's only one who I wish to meet,
Who once walked the earth on her own two feet,
She will come here now,
Let the whole world see,
How the humans bow,
How they worship me,
If she does not come,
If she will not kneel,
Then the Ocean Girl,
Will be my next meal!"

And the Turtle laughed,
"Are his brains all cheese?
I could kill them all,

With a magic sneeze,
I could boil their bones,
While I scratch my bum,
If he wills it so,
Then the girl will come,
For these Seas are hers,
And have always been,
Let our new Shark King meet the Ocean Queen."

"But it is safe to go?
Should we really dare?
What if it's a trap?
And when we get there,
He just eats me up,
What if that's his wish?
What if Ocean Girls are his favourite dish?"

"If on Ocean Girls, he desires to feed,
Then the new King's reign will be short indeed,
May he try his worst,
Let him do his best,
I will kill him first
And then all the rest of the sharks will die,
If they're even rude,
If they dare to think
You are Shark King food,
That you're
Yum! Yum! Yummy! Yummy!
Yum! Yum! Yum!
They'll be
Chum! Chum! Chummy! Chummy!
Chum! Chum! Chum!"

And so our little Chelly tried her best to feel brave,
And went down with the Turtle to that deep and darkest cave,
And as she swam down deeper she saw all the gathered sharks,

Saw their eyes and teeth all flashing in the all consuming dark,
But they didn't look so scary,
Like she'd thought they would before,
They watched her almost curiously,
Silently in awe.

"It is not what I expected."

And the Turtle gave a nod,

"I think something strange has happened here,
Really rather odd.
This new king must be fearsome,
For the sharks seem rather tamed,
Who is this shark who took their crown
though no one knew his name?"

And as they swam into his cave,
He spoke from on his throne,

"If you wouldn't mind,
I'd like to meet the Ocean Girl alone."

And the Turtle frowned so slightly,
But he bowed his scruffy head,

"The Shark King's word is law here,
But remember what I said!
All the Seas are yours,
And yours alone,
And one day you'll know why,
But for now, be wary of his words,
For sharks all love to lie."

And despite her pleas to stay,
He left her there in disbelief,
And she turned and faced the new Shark King,
Who grinned his razor teeth.

"So you are the girl they called Chellington Boots.
Who has tides for a pulse,
Coral for bones,
And seaweed for roots."

"That is I, as you say,
Who you summoned here,
Who comes now in peace..."

"And comes now in fear?"

"Do you want me to fear you?
To feel afraid?
Does fear make a king?"

"Fear is how kings are made.
Or to be more precise,
It's how kings keep their power,
Afraid to rise up,
All the masses will cower,
Will kneel and scrape,
Obsequious bows,
As kings ravage they make their subservient vows.
But not you, little Chelly,
Though I smell your fear,
Like one drop of blood fifty miles from here,
Though you tremble from head down to fancy new tail,
Though you shake like a jellyfish,

Quiver and quail,
You should not."

And the Shark King sat back with a smile.

"I wish only to chew on your ear for a while.
That is, to say, speak,
So please pardon the pun,
Please sit, you are safe here,
I'm honoured you've come."

"Tell me in what way has your honour been earned?
The tales of the Shark Kings, I've recently learned.
You're butchers,
You're beasts,
You're wicked and wild,
You pick meat from the bones of the tiniest child."

"Do you see any child?
Have I harmed you at all?
The sharks have learned much since they watched their King fall.
I am King now.
At least for the littlest of whiles.
And though sharks' teeth are sharp,
We still have pretty smiles.
I do not want this crown,
My own kingdom or cult,
But sharks bow to violence,
Or else they revolt,
But now they're in line,
For my word here is law,
There is nothing to fear from the sharks any more.
But tell me, little Chellyfish,
Girl whose grief and dying wish
Has brought her down here to the Seas,
Who swapped her thighs and calves and knees,
For scales and fins and fishy breath,

Was saved from her most lonesome death,
What magic do you have inside?
What makes you what you are?
Why would the Ocean Powers send the Turtle off so far?
You're just a girl,
I've met a few,
And you all look the same,
But for billions of years
The waves were whispering your name.
Though I took this throne the only way that thrones like this are won,
I'm afraid my reign must end though it has barely just begun.
The sharks are changing, Ocean Girl,
And you must help them learn,
It can't be me,
For there is something else for which I yearn,
There's a war that I've seen coming,
That will start above the Sea,
But I can't fight without your help,
The spell's too big for me."

"I don't know what you're asking,
What do you want me to do?
I'm just a girl, I have no power,
What use am I to you?"

"You have all the power in this world,
I see now in your eyes!
I hear it in the words you speak,
That flame like fireflies!
That fly like dragons!
Roll like thunder!
Shape the Seas and lands!
I had to meet you,
Now I know,
My future's in your hands."

"What magic do you ask of me?"

"I want to be a man!
To walk beneath the starry skies like only humans can,
There are bad things that are coming,
You must give me lungs and feet,
To go up there where there is air..."

"And tasty kids to eat!
What makes you think I'd help you?
That I'd trust a thing you say?
For all I know, your words are lies!"

"There is no other way!
Look here!
All the children that the sharks have brought to me!
They're safe and sound,
Not one hair harmed,
And I will set them free.
Believe me, little Ocean Girl,
You have to understand!
If you had seen the things I've seen...
My fate is on the land!"

"What is that you say you've seen?
What troubles are to come?

Down here we only belch and burp,
Blow bubbles just for fun!"

"This world of yours is make believe!
Though you choose not to see!
But you must open up your eyes,
Become what you must be!
There is something that is stirring,
That will rise up from the deep,
When the Oceans need their Ocean Girl,
She can't be half asleep!
I have smelled..
Blood.
So much blood, little Ocean Girl.
So much blood.
And I have heard,
Such sounds.
Sounds that you cannot imagine.
I've heard the buzzing of cancerous flies,
Seen maggots in sockets where there should be eyes,
And blisters all burst,
All seeping and sore,
Pestilent, putrid and rabidly raw.
I have seen...
War.
Malice and murder unheard of before."

"Up there?" Chelly whispered.

"And here in the Sea.
But if you wake up,
There's no need here for me!"

"Well, you finally talk truth!
For the first time today!"

And the Turtle who'd snuck up in some secret way was beside her,

"What nonsense this new Shark King speaks,
If your tale was a boat, it would certainly leak,
It has even more holes than a sea sponge's bum!
They said you were different but you're just as dumb as the King
you supplanted,
And all before him,
Though a tad more creative,
You're equally dim!
What a chest of old chestnuts,
Of fancy and fluff!
It's time we were leaving,
We've heard quite enough!"

"And what are you, Turtle?
A fool in a shell!
You have no real power,
And that's just as well,
For as dumb as you are,
You are twice as much vain!
Because you've seen the past where you dance in the rain?
It's her with the power to face what will come!
But she is not ready for what must be done!
I have seen it all, Turtle,
And you've seen it too!
The Seas will all rot while she's rescuing you!
I am telling you, Ocean Girl,
I do not lie!
But if you don't change me,
These children will die!
I will let them all die!
You will watch them all die!
You must change me, Chellyfish,
No one but I..."

But just as he spoke, he rebounded a spell,
That whammied the Turtle half out of his shell!

"Your magic's pathetic,
A childish charm,
I don't want to fight you or cause any harm!"

"He is lying!"

"They're dying!
Their faces are blue!"

And Chellyfish cried,
"What you ask, I will do!"
Now release them!"

And she looked him square in his eye.

"But next time we meet,
If this all was a lie,
I make you this promise,
I swear on the Seas,
If I give you ankles and elbows and knees,
And you use them for murder,
Then this much is true,
That you will die screaming,
While I smile at you."

And she felt a stirring deep down in her veins
That felt like the sound that your hear when it rains
And the shark king had hands where before he'd had fins,
Where once there were gills there was now only skin,
And he gathered the children up in his new arms,
"I give you my word, they will come to no harm,
But a Shadow is coming,
And you must beware!"

And with a Pop! and a Hom!
He was no longer there.

But Chellyfish that night could not sleep a wink,

She tossed and turned

And turned and tossed

And could not help but think.

"He spoke of some approaching death,
A Shadow that would suck the breath,
The joy, the life, from out the Seas
Destroy the world, if not for me,
But who am I?
I'm just a girl!"

"A girl like none before!"

And the Turtle who had come to save her,
Knocked upon her door,
Took her hand and pulled her close,
And stared into her eyes,

"There is no start there is no end,
There is no life that dies,
The present moment, never past,
That never starts, forever lasts."

And down there in the silent sea
He held her tightly.

"Look at me!
You're right where you're supposed to be,
No danger here,
No fear,
For we will be together all our days,
The waves are whistling songs of praise,
The heavens swear we cannot die,

For up there in the endless sky,
The planets cartwheel with the stars,
Orion's Belt is twirling Mars,
The Universe is grinning wide,
The winds are dancing with the tides,
So smile my love,
And dry your eyes,
We're off to play with butterflies."

But a thousand miles away there was a wave that hit a rock,
And clinging to it,
Breathing deeply,
Half in awe and shock,
A brand new man,
Just newly born,
Looked up into the sky,

"So this is where the people live,
And soon where they will die!"

The Girl Who Makes The World

"If the tales are true, he's found her."

"Old those stories are.
Who knows what wise old whelk or winkle dreamed them up
afar,
In Seas a million miles away,
In times a billion years ago.
Is this the girl who makes the world?
There's only you who'd know."

"I'm afraid that's not the way it works,
It's not for me to see,
Nothing's sure,
The past's a blur,
The future's yet to be."

"You say it's not for you to see,
But I have seen it so,
Where she'll face the Shadow,
I have no such power to know,
But I have seen her angry,
And of this I have no doubt,

That if Father Time betrays her,
She will tear his insides out."

And they sat a while in silence,
And the Shark King felt it all,
Saw the rustle of palm leaves,
And heard the birds call,
Felt the wind on his fingers,
And tasted the air,
That smelled like the salt in the Ocean Girl's hair.

"You know, that there are kings up here,
Whose kingdoms never end,
Who cause such pain and suffering its impossible to mend,
Who crush their people under them!
Rape the women,
Slaughter men..."

"And you intend to rescue them?
To overthrow those kings?
And then...?
The Oceans are in peril,
And the Shark King runs away."

"The Oceans have an Ocean Girl,
No need for me to stay."

"An Ocean Girl who has such power,
She cannot comprehend!"

"And what are you who speaks for her?
Who act like you're her friend?!
I have dreamed!
Of shadows and shipwrecks and screams!
And I know that Time is not all that he seems!
A shadow stalks the Ocean Girl,
A shadow she will face,

That I have seen her face alone in the loneliest place.
I have not seen Father Time come rushing to her aid.
All you have is words,
And empty oaths that you have made."

"What oaths have I broken?
What lies have I told?"

"That all things must die after all things get old.
But you have not died yet.
You break your own rule,
And you put that girl's fate in the hands of a fool,
He's seen it as I have,
But he laughs and grins,
And watches her fight when there's no way she'll win."

"And that's nothing to you?
Does the Shark King not care?
The Turtle would kill just for harming a
hair on the head of that girl."

"Then why does he not?
I've seen the Turtle when Seas start to rot,
When Oceans decay,
When reefs are all black,
He fears what he sees, so he's turning his back.
The Shadow brings Death,
It's a funeral song,
And the Turtle is deaf but still whistling along."

"He doesn't mean ill,
He thinks she's so strong."

"Let's hope that he's right,
We're all dead if he's wrong."

"Your lives are the blink of the blink of an eye,
Alive for the moment,

The next one you die."

"So speaks the wise and the all-knowing Time,
But the fact you exist has no reason or rhyme,
I don't know what you are,
But I know one thing is true,
That all wise men agree that there is no such thing as you."

"All wise men agree?
Tell me, have you met such a thing?
A man who could see that beyond the hairs upon his chin?
Perhaps you'll meet one up here,
Or perhaps you'll be the first,
Will a shark become the best of men,
Or will he be the worst?"

"Enough of your riddles.
Enough of your words.
I have ears now only for breezes and birds.
My eyes must look up,
I must walk on the sand,
The Seas are behind me,
Before me, the land.
So spare me your lectures,
Deny me your lies,
This shark's now a man of the shores and the skies.
Farewell old destroyer,
We won't meet again,
Watch out for the girl who will dance in the rain."

And a little while later, if you went up to a mighty cliff,
You'd find a turtle frightened stiff,
And his three friends who told him,

"If we're careful this time…"

"…there's no harm…"

"…no broken legs or broken arms…"

"…and if there are.."

"…then Chellyfish can fix them with her magic charms…"

"…just like before…"

"…so no harm done…"

"Come quickly now,
Before the sun wakes them all up,
Before the morning,
Foils our plan,
And spoils our fun!"

"Okay, now, ready,
One!
Aaaaaaaaaand

Two!
Aaaaaaand…!"

"Goodness, what a great big boulder,
Gosh, that's such a giant rock…"

"It's Chelly!"
They all gasped in shock,

"…that you're all trying so hard to block,
And fully failing now to hide,
And who is this who's popped inside his little shell?
Can it be so?"

"We're sorry, Chelly!"

"Please don't go and tell the Turtle what we've done!"

"We're only trying to have some fun!"

"Don't snitch on us!"

"Don't tattle-tale!"

"Don't spill the beans to everyone!"

And Chelly, smiling, made the oath,

"Now that you've implicated me…

…No other way that I can see…

Okay then ready?

One!

Two!

Three!"

MICHAEL FEGAN

Made in the USA
Columbia, SC
22 December 2020